This Ladybird Book belongs to:

_____

_____

_____

_____

Ladybird

*This Ladybird retelling*
*by*
*Joan Stimson*

Published by Ladybird Books Ltd
80 Strand London WC2R 0RL
A Penguin Company
13 15 17 19 20 18 16 14 12
© LADYBIRD BOOKS LTD 1993

Printed in Italy

FAVOURITE TALES

# The Three Billy Goats Gruff

*illustrated*
*by*
*CHRIS RUSSELL*

*based on a traditional folk tale*

Once upon a time there were three billy goats called Gruff. One day, they set off in search of some sweet, green grass.

Very soon the goats came to a river. Across the river there was a meadow, and in the meadow grew the finest grass that any of them had ever seen.

Now, there was a wooden bridge over the river, and under this bridge lived a *very* fierce and ugly troll. Every time he heard footsteps going *trip, trap, trip, trap,* across the bridge, he jumped out and gobbled up whoever was trying to cross.

The three billy goats Gruff were very frightened of the troll, but they still longed to eat the sweet, green grass.

After a while the youngest billy goat Gruff stepped forward. "I'm tired of waiting," he said. "I will try to cross the bridge."

*Trip, trap, trip, trap,* went the little goat's hooves on the wooden planks. Soon he was halfway across.

Suddenly, *up* popped the ugly troll! "Who's that trip-trapping over *my* bridge?" he roared.

"It's only me… the littlest billy goat Gruff," said the frightened goat in a tiny voice. "I'm off to the meadow to eat the green grass."

"Then I'm coming to gobble you up!" roared the troll.

"Oh, *please* don't gobble me up," said the youngest billy goat Gruff. "Wait until the second billy goat Gruff comes along. He's much fatter than I am."

And the youngest billy goat Gruff crossed the bridge and skipped off into the meadow to eat the sweet, green grass.

Then the second billy goat Gruff stepped forward. "Now I will try to cross the bridge," he said.

*Trip, trap, trip, trap,* went his hooves on the wooden planks. Soon he was halfway across.

Suddenly, *up* popped the ugly troll! "Who's that trip-trapping over *my* bridge?" he roared.

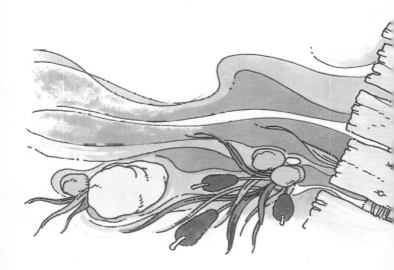

"It's only me… the second billy goat Gruff," said the goat. "I'm off to the meadow to eat the green grass."

"Then I'm going to gobble you up!" roared the troll.

"Oh, *please* don't gobble me up," said the second billy goat Gruff. "Wait until the third billy goat Gruff comes along. He's *very* big and fat!"

And the second billy goat Gruff
crossed the bridge and skipped
off into the meadow to eat the
sweet, green grass.

At last the biggest billy goat Gruff decided to cross the bridge.

*Trip, trap, trip, trap, bang, bang, bang, bang!* went his hooves on the wooden planks, until he was halfway across the bridge.

Suddenly, *up* popped the ugly troll!

"Who's that trip-trapping over *my* bridge?" roared the troll.

"It's me… the biggest billy goat Gruff," said the goat in his loud, gruff voice. "I'm off to the meadow to eat the green grass."

"Then I'm coming to gobble you up!" roared the troll.

"Oh no, you're not!" bellowed the biggest billy goat Gruff. "I'M COMING TO GOBBLE *YOU* UP!"

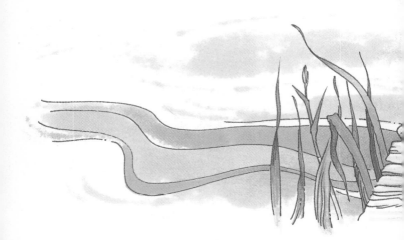

Then the biggest billy goat Gruff
lowered his mighty horns and
thundered towards the troll. *Trip,
trap, trip, trap, bang, bang, BANG,
BANG!*

He butted the ugly troll high into
the air.

*SPLASH!* The troll fell down and down, head first into the deep water. The river rushed on, carrying the troll far, far away.

The biggest billy goat Gruff smiled to himself and skipped off into the meadow to eat the sweet, green grass.

The ugly troll was never seen again. And from that day on, no one was afraid to cross the bridge.

As for the three billy goats Gruff, they all ate so much sweet, green grass that they grew into very fat billy goats indeed!